I0606913

Anonymous

Rhymes

Anonymous

Rhymes

ISBN/EAN: 9783337391850

Printed in Europe, USA, Canada, Australia, Japan

Cover: Foto ©Andreas Hilbeck / pixelio.de

More available books at **www.hansebooks.com**

RHYMES

BY

KENAWMEN

Tʜᴇsᴇ sᴛᴀɴᴢᴀs have been written, mostly, for Mission Sunday School Celebrations and Young Peoples Meetings.

At the request of some friends they are now printed with the hope that they may prove a source of pleasure and profit to the boys and girls of the Sunday Schools and Religious Societies.

Kᴇɴᴀᴡᴍᴇɴ.

Fort Washington, Pa., 1892.

Entered according to Act of Congress
in the Office of the Librarian of Congress at Washington, D C.
A. D. 1892.

A BUNCH OF KEYS.

I know some little boys
Who love to make a noise
With fife and drum and toys.
                    So they do!

I've hit upon a plan
To help each little man
To do the best he can
                    To be true!

I have a bunch of keys:
Now listen, if you please,
What I will say of these;
                    Look at me!

These keys are on a ring;
For that's the very thing,
Much better than a string,
                    For a key!

This key is for the door
To knowledge, truth and lore
And mines of hidden ore
                    Stored away!

Why need I to explain?
This key unlocks the brain
Or locks it up.—that's plain,
                    Plain as ".A".

3

7.

Now. here's another key !
'Tis very clear to me,
I think you all can see
       What I mean ;
The closet of our hearts
Has many secret parts ;
· This key emotion starts ;
       So be keen !

It needs no little skill
To tell the good from ill
Or manage one's own will,
       As you see ;
The good you should let in,
But keep out every sin ;
This key will help you win
       Victory !

With knowledge fill your brain,
Your heart's affection train,
Your will's control maintain
       All your days !

I hope you will agree
Aright to use each key.
Then you shall happy be
       Be always !

4

NOTHING TO DO.

Nothing to do! Who could have uttered these words?
The diligent insects, the swift fleeing birds?
The ocean that's rolling on day after day,
Or time in its flight, not a moment to stay?

Nothing to do! And so much work to be done;
Where sinners are perishing; souls to be won!
The armies of Satan are still in the field,
And earth's timid pilgrims stand willing to yield.

Nothing to do! In the great harbors of sin,
With the ebb going out and flood coming in.
The work of destruction is marching apace,
Though Mercy is pleading and offering grace.

Nothing to do! Are there no prizes to gain,
When others are fighting their crowns to obtain?
Up, up, and be doing, work while it is day.
The minutes are passing too swiftly away.

Nothing to do! In this glad noontide of light,
Thank God for thy talents, strike out for the right!
Perform with a will what thy hands find to do.
Arise to thy duty, be faithful and true.

Nothing to do! In yon bright haven above
Where Jesus stands welcoming sinners with love,
When conflicts are over, thy last battle won.
Thy toils shall be ended, thy resting begun.

POLITENESS.

He who is not clever to me
May not be kind to my brother;
The test of good manners, you see,
Is,—how do you treat one another.

I like a good shake of the hand,
At least a slight recognition;
It certainly pays to bland
Much more than to flaunt erudition.

Politeness costs little, you know,
Yet yields returns so abundant
That those who received it bestow
Quite often their plaudits redundant.

But never mind plaudits or thanks,
Just keep right on in the traces;
Leave ill-humored crosses for cranks
And cultivate heavenly graces.

'Tis noble a favor to grant
Where'er a service is needed;
Beware of all flattering cant,
For seldom false praises are heeded.

DO THE BEST.

What can be the use in repining o'er ills
That can't be avoided no matter who wills,
When life may be rendered so grandly sublime
By doing the very best every time.

Why mourn over trouble that never appears
And lengthen our days and thus shorten our years;
The rain with the sunshine should gladden the clime
When doing the very best every time.

Why bother with trifles or fret over loss,
The value of which may be nothing but dross;
Just keep the brain cool and the hands always prime,
Be ready to do the best every time.

Why suffer the weeds in the garden to grow
When flowers are struggling their beauties to show;
Go train lovely roses and woodbine to climb,
Keep doing the very best every time.

The clouds may be heavy but bright the sun shines
For light-heart no less than for him who repines;
So keep the soul guiltless from sorrow for crime
By doing the very best every time.

The days of this life will soon come to a close,
The spirit will enter its peaceful repose;
Then toll not the church-bell but ring a sweet chime
For him who has done his best every time.

POLLY'S PRECEPT.

A farmer, blest with strength and health,
Whose wife and children were his wealth,
That he might have his garner filled
His field with faithful labor tilled ;
A yoke of oxen stout and strong
Plowed o'er the furrows straight and long,
He harrowed all the ground, and more,
He rolled it level as a floor ;
And when the soil was thus prepared
With liberal hand the seed he shared,
So while the spring sun lit the morn
His field was planted well with corn.

The farmer's children, full of glee,
Had little time to disagree ;
But when they came to such a move
A family parrot would reprove
Their froward ways and silly words,
For, "Polly" was the best of birds ;
'Twas in its manners quite demure
And rudeness it could not endure ;
It had its freedom in the home
And sometimes on the lawn would roam,
It seldom sought the garden fence
Nor ventured far at most from thence.

One day at noon the farmer saw
A flock of crows and heard them "caw"
Down in the newly planted corn
Regardless of the "scare" to warn
Intruders. Quick as thought he springs
To where his trusty musket swings;
'Twas loaded ready for the game
Of beast or birdling, wild or tame.
He hastened to the nether porch,
And vowed their feathers he would scorch;
No sooner said than it was done,
"Bang"! went the farmer's faithful gun.

As presently the smoke arose
It showed destruction 'mongst the crows;
An observation shortly found
A dozen dead lay on the ground;
But, what surprised the farmer most,
The favored parrot, midst the host,
Lay fretting o'er its sorry lot,
For, with the crows it had been shot;
Its leg was broken, sad to tell,
And needed to be splintered well;
The farmer placed it to his breast
And took it back to its own nest.

" Alas! Alas!" the yeoman said,
"What mischief ever filled your head
To dare to join those thieving crows?"

9

No sin without demerit goes.
"Bad company!" the farmer cried,
"Bad company!" poor Poll replied.
'Twas curiosity at first
That gave the parrot such a thirst
To form acquaintance,—mingling in
With others who led on to sin.
So soon the penalty was paid
And Polly near death's door was laid!

At last the wound was slowly healed
And Polly's wisdom was revealed,
Enough, at least, to warn its friends
Against temptation's hurtful ends.
Well may it dread the woeful day
It wandered from its home away!
Bad company it now eschews,
Nor spares its voice to sound the news
Whene'er it thinks the duty plain
Some neighbors children to restrain;
For at the least discrepancy
Poll fiercely shouts, "Bad company!"

If Poll with home had been content
'Twould have no reason to relent
The sad misfortune that befell
On this occasion. But 'twas well
For all: for now it knows
How trouble with bad friendship goes

And Poll will always be concerned
To teach the lesson that it learned.
(The lesson that's so full of truth.)
To children dear and blooming youth:
Who well their daily course would run
Bad company must ever shun.

BIRDIE.

Pretty little bird sitting in the tree,
What have you to say to me?
Pretty birdie sings from a bough above,
" Cheer up, dearie! cheer up, love!"

Pretty little birds, sweetly you agree
Up in yonder maple tree!
Darling children here never should be sad;
Sing like birdies, all be glad.

Little folks, like birds, ever should delight
All day long to do the right;
Birdies sweetly sing anthems in the air,
Children too, their joy may share.

Precious children may, like the birdies, bring
Sweetest songs to Christ our King.
Tiny little birds ever have God's care,
He loves children everywhere.

Little birdie dear, one more word with you ;
May be God loves big folks too ?
I am glad in this you and I agree :
Truly, God loves you and me.

SABBATH MORNING.

The distant Church-bell's soft sweet sound
    Floats o'er the hill so clear.
And lovely echoes linger 'round,
    Delightful to the ear.

The early call to prayer and praise
    Should claim our earnest heed ;
Affection's tribute should we raise
    To our best Friend in need.

Oh, quiet peace of Sabbath morn !
    The herds stand 'neath the shade,
The silent fields of ripened corn,
    The brook beyond the glade,

The wooded landscape and the mill,
    And there the aftermath,
All nature hushed ; so very still
    Along the quaint old path.

The autumn sun, with rays so sheen,
    Drives frost and cloud away,
Adds life and beauty to the scene
    So restful yet so gay.

The plowman's teams are in the stalls,
    The sheep are by their cotes,
The robins sing their matin calls,
    The larks their cheery notes ;

Thus, nature seems to own the day
    And honor God indeed.
And with ten thousand tongues to say
    Anew her holy creed.

HOW LITTLE WE KNOW.

The earth with its mountains and valleys and seas,
Its lakes and its islands and forests of trees,
The heated equator, the ice at the poles,
The lightning's sharp flash as the loud thunder rolls,
The seed-time and harvest, then winter and snow,
But lo ! of creation how little we know !

The mountains so high and the oceans so wide,
Volcanoes with lava-lined craters inside,
The tides that forever and aye ebb and flow,
The clouds in the heavens, the sunshine and bow,
The earthquakes the maelstroms, the cyclones that blow,
All teach us the lesson : how little we know !

The sun 'midst the azure, that great fiery ball,
Of stars in their Kingdom seems monarch of all;
With power unseen our fair planet is held
By solar attraction! And we are compelled
To ponder and wonder, as days come and go,
How much we behold but how little we know!

Those stars shining o'er us so bright in the skies
For ages have baffled the skill of the wise!
Pray, can they be peopled with folk such as we?
Astronomers millions would give just to see!
Now, telescopes bring distant worlds to our view
And suns are discovered the sages ne'er knew.

The moon sheds on earth its reflected pale light,
A comet perchance may be wheeled into sight.
Bright meteors shoot through etherial space,
The galaxy's myriads each in its place;
These wonders in heavens and earth ever show
How much is to learn and how little we know.

Great mines under ground full of mineral ore,
Broad prairies abounding in generous store
Of grain for the millions, for man and for beast;
And fountains of waters, of blessings not least,
A bountiful God who, in earth, sea and air,
Provides for His creatures with Fatherly care.

14

Though much we may know yet far more is to learn;
The way up to knowledge has many a turn.
The earth and the sun, moon and stars may appear
To us all of knowledge that's worth knowing here;
But shall we not study our joys to increase?
The path of truth wisdom leads onward to peace.

The Lord has revealed through the Book of His grace
Some gleams of His glory, some light from His face;
And searchers for truth will assuredly find
God's Word is a lamp that enlightens the mind,
And things quite unseen by faith we may know
E'en here while we journey 'midst darkness and woe.

Rich treasures, and pleasures that ne'er can be told,
And blessings unmeasured more precious than gold
The Lord has reserved for the Saints of His love,
Laid up in His Father-house waiting above.
What joys they inherit who serve Him below
None, none but the ransomed in Jesus can know.

WHAT FRUITAGE.

The minutes, hours, days and years
Fly onward fast with rapid wing
Through joys and sorrows, smiles and tears,
Life's buoyant hopes and anxious fears,
Till Jordan's brink so soon appears:
My soul, what fruitage wilt thou bring?

15

EASTER.

The Paschal Sacrifice is slain,
  And once for all the ransom paid;
The Temple veil is rent in twain,
  And Jesus in the tomb is laid.

But shall the grave yield up its dead?
  Will death release whom sin hath bound?
Yes, sin and death are captive led,
  And Jesus, Lord of Life, is crowned.

Hail holy day when Jesus rose
  Victorious over death and grave!
Hail blessed hope! Thrice happy those
  Whom Jesus died and rose to save.

Shall those who sleep in Jesus rise
  To everlasting life and peace?
Shall scenes of rapture fill their eyes
  And praise and blessing never cease?

Yes, they who in His name believe
  Shall rise and in his presence stand:
Fullness of joy shall they receive,
  And pleasure at their Lord's right hand.

Although their earthly house may mould,
  And mingle with its kindred clay,
They shall their risen Lord behold
  With perfect bliss in endless day.

Deliv'rance from the fear of woe
    Believers here rejoice to find ;
The sting of death they ne'er shall know,
    Nor can the grave their spirits bind.

Oh ! blest the hour when Jesus rose,
    When sin and death of pow'r were shorn !
Blest hour, which brought such sweet repose ;
    Oh, cherished Resurrection Morn !

THE CHRISTIAN'S MISSION.

Go tell the truth in love !
Go whisper to the downcast soul,
    How One who dwells above
Once died to make the sinner whole.   .

Go forth in love ! Prepare
The hardened soil and stony place,
    And scatter ev'rywhere
The Gospel seeds of Truth and Grace.

Go bring the wand'rer in !
Point to the road that leads away
    From paths of shame and sin,
And reaches up to endless day.

Go seek the erring one !
Lift up the Cross, and then confess
    What Christ for thee hath done ;
Thy sure reward ! Thy righteousness !

Go bless the suff'ring poor!
Show the kind Providential care
Of God! Whose word is sure
To all who come in trustful prayer.

Go comfort those who mourn,
With words of love! For weary man,
The tempest tossed and torn,
Christ bled and died and lives again.

HOME.

Blest home! may thy glad mem'ries cheer
My path upon this mundane sphere:
No purer joys can e'er arise
'Twixt thy fond hearth and yonder skies.

My wayward feet perchance may roam
From thee, my childhood's Heaven-blest home·
Yet may thy influence sweet abide
To soothe my sorrows, check my pride.

Bright emblem of my home above
I'll cherish still thy bond of love,
'Til in my Father's House I rest
With those I know and love the best.

THE FUTURE.

Thou knowest not, my dear one,
What trials thou shalt bear ;
A veil the future hideth
With all its woe and care.

I would not wish to open
More than a single page
Of what shall be transacted
Within the coming age.

But, page by page unfolding,
The future comes in view,
And shows each generation
Its longings, false or true.

The book of nature ever
Is wise and good and pure,
And he who seeketh knowledge
Will find its counsel sure.

The past hath clearly taught us
The present to employ ;
The seed-time gone, the harvest
May bring us fruits of joy.

But should the storm-wind scatter
Thy prospects in a day,
Have courage for the morrow
To drive thy cares away.

The dangers in thy pathway,
The sorrows, pains and fears,
May fade before the sun-light
Of thy declining years.

Then, when the earth-shades lengthen,
Thy day draws to its close,
May God thy spirit strengthen
And give thee sweet repose.

"MAKING THE MOST OF LIFE."

Whate'er the duty you begin.
Do your best !
What faithful service cannot win.
Leave the rest !
The times are often out of joint
More or less !
Good friends may sometime disappoint ;
Forward press !
 Strive, strive to conquer every task.
 Nor stop to argue or to ask
 Why blessings come beneath a mask ;
  What nearest to your path may lie
  Do well your part ! You sure can try !
  Success may crown you bye and bye,
     Bye and bye !

PRESS ON.

The morning light illumes my path 'til near the short days end ;
The evening shows the loving hand of my most gracious Friend ;
The noontide hour the dial marks when I my powers should save,
And midnight points the period that lies beyond the grave.
Thus Time foretells all mortal things must swiftly pass away ;
Beyond the midnight comes the dawn of God's eternal day.
The morning of His glory bright shall shine upon me then.
Nor noontide sun nor midnight gloom shall e'er be known again.
The evening of my life draws near, my days are well nigh spent,
How precious should each day appear as each by Heaven is lent ;
So, may I press with holy zeal to reach the gladsome prize
And fix my faith and love on Him who reigns above the skies.

" KIND WORDS NEVER DIE. "

Be courteous and kind to the people you meet
In palace or hovel, in workshop or street :
You never may know how one sweet gentle word
To heavenly action some frail heart has stirred.

Example is golden and precept has weight
In character building, or forming a state ;
But one gentle word that is spoken in love
Sends an echo that's welcomed by angels above.

THE CONSOLATION OF ISRAEL.

The night of sin has cast its gloom
   O'er Judah's hills and valleys fair;
A nation hastens to her doom,
   Her priests and scribes have proved h r snare.
The darkness deepens! Wider'spreads
   Her desolation everywhere!
A foreign foe now proudly treads
   Her highways; rears his standard there.
Jerusalem! Thy prophets slain!
   Thy broken law! Thy sin revealed!
Self-righteous, superstitious, vain;
   Thy sceptre thou hast ceased to wield.

Thy Temple, like a lone star, stands
   An emblem of God's truth and grace;
A beacon bright to far-off lands;
   To it the captive turns his face.
Its altar stained by rebel bands
   Whose murd'rous deeds pollute the place,
While greedy men with guilty hands
   In changing gold its courts disgrace.
The homage due thy Sov'reign God
   Is laid aside for empty show;
'Neath haughty Caesar's lash and rod
   A harder service must thou know.

O, Zion's Daughter, hast thou mourned
  Thy heavy burden? Thy dark night?
Hast thou yet heeded those who warned
  Thee of the sword and bitter flight,
When alien hosts, (once by thee scorned,)
  Should thy rich fields and vineyards blight?
Or, by God's promises adorned,
  Wilt hie thee to the dawning Light?
Come, listen then, expectant look
  To promised Bethlehem's sacred height!
Let sage and shepherd search the Book
  And find a Saviour clothed with might.

Sweet joy of comfort! Bond of love!
  A God comes down to dwell on earth!
He leaves the glory, had above,
  With men to live! His humble birth
Announced by star! When quickly move
  The wise men from their distant land;
And shepherd's by their actions prove
  Their rev'rence for a Prince so grand!
The Light now shines o'er grove and plain;
  Kings' palaces and halls of lore,
Evangeled by this glorious reign,
  Resound with praises evermore.

Old Simeon long may wait, 'til years
  Shall tell his days are growing few;
But hope he mingles with his tears
  And prays for strength to see the true
Salvation dawn.   Lo, it appears!
  In peace he dies, his journey through.
And aged Anna gladly cheers
  The longing heart of pious Jew.
Who, of the Consolation hears
  With joyous faith and feelings new,
Dispels his doubts, casts off his fears,
  Since his Messiah is in view.

Oh, precious Light! Oh, glorious Sun
  Of Righteousness!   Thy truth and grace
By ancient seer foretold! Blest One
  Who pardon brings to all our race!
Thou Hope of Israel!   May we run
  To Thee for help, and in Thee trace
Our full salvation! Holy Son,
  The Image of the Father's face,
We bless Thee for the victory won
  By Thee for us!   Let nought displace
Our trust 'til life's brief journey's done
  And we are safe in Thy embrace.

FLOWERS AND FANCIES.

Flowers and fancies crowd upon my brain.
Though covered o'er with ice and snow the plain ;
Flowers forever live with perfume fresh,
While fancies are not children of the flesh.

Flowers in mem'ry bloom and bloom again
With sweeter fragrance, brighter hues than when
Hours of sadness, solitude and grief
Forbade these tender joys their sweet relief.

Buttercup and daisy o'er the field,
Both rich in love and innocence, they yield
Pleasures pure and lasting, noble, strong,
To give the spirit power to conquer wrong.

Youth with loving charms the primrose brings,
With lilacs to enforce the thought that springs
Blythe and free from hearts so warm and true,
And woodbine sparkling wet with morning dew.

Whence the feelings through these trifles wrought?
No trifle this arbutus ! that was brought
Miles on miles, from distant woods where grew
The honeysuckle wild and violet blue.

Years have sped their course and left behind
Indelible impressions on the mind !
Gone the bloom of youth ! Maturer age
Bids busy care the riper thought engage.

Fancy stronger grows as sets our sun
When we remember kindly actions don ;
Parted now from dearest earthly friends
Blest Hope a bright anticipation lends.

Heads of hoary whiteness pass along
Scarce mingling with the noisy active throng;
Each a burden bears 'midst doubt and fears,
And patient Faith may wipe away their tears.

Closer bind the sympathetic chord
'Twixt man and man ! The blessing of the Lord
Ever rests on such as willing share
With those who through affliction sadly fare.

Wait then not the coffin lid to close
O'er those we love when in their last repose ;
Garlands bring of flowers while life is warm,
'Twill help our brother brave the fiercest storm.

MEMORIAL DAY.

God bless Memorial Day !
May Peace her sceptre sway
        O'er our broad Land !
Fond mem'ry's sacred seal
Set for the Nation's weal,
Day fraught with holy zeal,
        Hand joined to hand.

Glad day when comrades meet
And brethren kindly greet,
                    Voice echoes voice ;
Sweet music fills the air.
Bells ringing everywhere,
Heart answers heart in prayer
                    While all rejoice.

On scenes of joy and love
Look angels from above,
                    Smiling on Peace !
Firm bound by Freedom's ties
In God our host relies ;
To Him let praise arise,
                    Our faith increase !

No more let cannon roar !
Reign Peace from shore to shore
                    'Til end of days !
Thy guiding grace afford.
Unite with one accord
This mighty Nation, Lord,
                    Thy Name to praise !

When children's children say.
" What means Memorial Day
                    In this blest Land ? "
Let sire to son relate
How God, in mercy great.
With honor saved the State.
                    A Union grand.

′A SENTIMENT.

With all their meaning words may fail to dress
In proper form that clearly will express
The cherished thought that seeks the light of day
Which long has lain within the mind away.

Some words are written, others sung or said,
All wise or senseless as the heart or head
From which they spring.   What sounds are these we hear
That bless or curse, applaud, or fill with fear!

Sweet melody of birds in thicket green
Where brooks ring harmonies the rocks between!
The organ's solemn peal, the zither's air!
No music can with human voice compare.

The whistle shrill or moan of winter's blast,
The crash of tree by tempest earthward cast,
Nor less the ear is struck with anxious dread
When marred by words of strife with passion fed.

Like golden apples laid on silver bright
Are words of wisdom when they're said aright;
One utterance a wounded heart may heal
And life eternal in that word reveal.

The sympathizing breast will sometime swell
With loving sentiments that rise to quell
The sinner's fear, his unbelief o'erthrow;
A faithful word may save a life of woe.

The soul beneath and through the living word
Speaks in mysterious influence, unheard
Within the realm of nature all profound,
And echoes forth God's praise in glory sound.

AT BETHANY.

When Jesus rested on the way,
'Twas Mary's choice by Him to stay
While Martha served throughout the day
           At Bethany.

Friend Lazarus, whose goods were few.
The precious love of Jesus knew ;
No dwarfed affection ever grew
           At Bethany.

As from Jerusalem He went.
To save the sons of men intent.
Full many Sabbaths Jesus spent
           At Bethany.

Rich Simon for his royal guest
In sumptuous feast spared not his best ·
And Mary's faith was put to test
           At Bethany.

The costly spikenard filled the air
With perfume sweet : 'Twas Mary's hair
That wiped the feet of Jesus there,
               At Bethany.

O may our weary footsteps turn
The good to seek, the ill to spurn ;
Life's grandest lessons well to learn
               At Bethany.

To Christ God's faithful ones are known,
Until the end he loves his own.
His power in earth and heaven was shown
               At Bethany.

HARVEST HOME.

Crowned with mercies ! Blest, and well supplied
With earthly good, our needs are satisfied.
Thanks and praise to God are justly due
For benefits and blessings ever new.

Providence has spread with open hand
The harvest in profusion o'er the land ;
Barns are filled with grain and fruits abound.
Dire want has fled and plenty reigns around.

Countless millions with their daily bread
By wondrous pow'r and loving grace are fed;
Gratitude now bends the humble knee
For products of the field so rich and free.

Year by year the seasons come and go,
With Summer's radiant heat and Winter's snow;
Seed-time blithe, then harvest's golden days,
Inviting man his Maker's name to praise.

Southward moves the sun to shed its powers
In other climes, on other fields than ours;
Moon and stars their annual course pursue,
And heaven rules the wind. the rain, the dew.

Autumn paints the wood with brilliant hues,
The meads and uplands yield enchanting views;
Nature dons th' attire of jubilee,
And Nature's God is seen through herb and tree.

Thanks we render for these blessings sent
As gifts rewarding man for labor spent.
Toil is man's, with sweat he turns the sod;
'Tis ours to sow. the harvest comes from God.

May sorrow never thee oppress.
Thy days be blest with happiness;
Let love for thee its garlands 'twine
And sweetest peace be ever thine.

                              My Valentine.

A PLEA FOR WORK.

I've come in search of labor.
   Just something light to do.
I've neither kin nor neighbor
   Who cares to help me through.

I've ne'er, sir, a profession.
   Nor ever learned a trade ;
To make a clean confession,
   I am a renegade.

For books I've had no liking.
   From school I truant played.
No thought my mind e'er striking
   The blunder I had made.

My ways were downward tending,
   With none but self to blame,
When, 'most too late for mending,
   Sad days of hardship came.

My meals, sir, in the morning.
   Are never quite in view,
'Til I, my patches scorning,
   Secure a job or two.

I sometimes get a dinner,
   It may be cold or warm,
Enough for such a sinner
   Who's trying to reform.

I've found for each night's lodging
　　It's hard to raise the pay !
It keeps me always dodging
　　To find a place to stay.

You ask me where I staid, sir?
　　Last night I had a cot,
'Twas fifteen cents I paid, sir,
　　To sleep among a lot

Of filthy, ugly creatures
　　Who came from every land ;
You should have seen their features !
　　'Twas more than I could stand.

I never could endure, sir,
　　That crew another night
If I could but procure, sir,
　　Some easy job at sight.

No one can call me lazy,
　　I'm supple and I'm sound ;
It sets me nearly crazy
　　To think I've run aground.

I've waited now already
　　For work to come along
Almost a fortnight steady,
　　'Tis still the same old song !

The times are somewhat tighter
　　Than, say, a year ago;
I hope they'll soon be brighter,
　　That I may have some show.

No lane was e'er so long, sir,
　　That never had a turn:
I trust I'll not go wrong, sir,
　　I'm not too old to learn!

No miracle, whatever!
　　A man of me 'twould make
If some one would endeavor
　　My case to undertake.

I'd never, sir, forget it.
　　I'd faithful prove to be;
And you would ne'er regret
　　If you'd once tie to me.

But if you can't employ me
　　I must apply elsewhere;
It surely does annoy me
　　To meet such wretched fare.

I'm certain someone wants me
　　To show or pack their goods;
Somehow, the idea haunts me,
　　I'll soon get through the woods.

I thank you for this pittance ;
　　I'm good for one more night !
I may get a remittance
　　And make it up all right.

Excuse me, sir, for pressing
　　In busy hours my plea :
'Tis really, sir, distressing.
　　There seems no luck for me !

Another day is coming.
　　Again I'll try the chase :
For I'm just tired of bumming
　　Around from place to place.

FIELD FLOWERS.

Flowers by the brooklet. blue and pink and white;
Flowers o'er the meadow. what a pretty sight !
Scarce a green-house flower can at all compare
With these beauties of the field scattered everywhere
Some exotic gathered in a foreign land.
E'en a prickly cactus growing in the sand,
Strikes. perchance, our fancy and enchantment lends.
But in time our love comes back for our dear old friends.

35

THOUGHTS ON A LESSON.

We sit at the end of a Sabbath-day's rest.
The sun has gone down o'er the hills of the west;
We think of the home that is surely the best,
That glorious home in the realms of the blest.

Though birds had their nests and foxes their caves,
No home had the Saviour!   The Jesus who saves!
The Jesus who stilleth wild Galilee's waves!
Who calmeth sin's tempests, while Satan yet raves.

Our hearts' best affections, in glad sacrifice,
We lay at his altar.   He rescued from vice
Our guilt-laden souls.   Now His blood can suffice
For all our transgressions, free, free of all price.

We render Him humbly our portion of praise:
His Name be our song 'til the end of our days.
We long to behold Him. with silent amaze:
On Him who was slain we would wond'ringly gaze.

With Heavenly wisdom divinely He taught;
His words and His actions were constantly fraught
With love for poor sinners, whose welfare He sought,
Whose pardon on Calvary's Cross He has bought.

Compassion He had on the thousands He fed;
Salvation He gave them as freely as bread.
To life He restores wretched souls that were dead;
Oh glorify Jesus, the Christian's great Head!

Rejoice and be thankful for what He has done;
The blessed Lord Jesus. the Father's dear Son!
The Kingdom of Heaven on earth has begun
Since vict'ry o'er sin and the grave He hath won.

Triumphant in Heaven His great army brings
Oblations of praise; while the Church grandly sings
Its anthems of glory, as time its flight wings,
To Jesus the Lord. ever King over Kings.

At home with our Saviour, Redeemer and Friend!
At rest in His presence on whom we depend!
We'll wait for His summons, then promptly attend,
To be with our Lord in the world without end.

HAPPINESS.

To make the best of life while here,
To scatter blessings far and near,
To drop the sympathizing tear
            For those who comfort need;
To fill sad hearts with gladsome cheer
And be content within the sphere
Of daily duty through the year,
            Is happiness indeed.

OLD GLORY.

Old Glory swings out to the breeze
  From the staff at the top of the hill.
Her colors gleam high o'er the trees;
  Let us cheer with a hearty good will!

        Hurrah! Hurrah! Hurrah!
          Old Glory's the flag of the free.
        Hurrah! Hurrah! Hurrah!
          Old Glory's the flag for me.

Old Glory crowns mountain and vale
  With her stars and her stripes wide unfurled,
America's ensign we hail!
  She's a beacon of hope to the world.
        Hurrah! Hurrah! Hurrah!

Old Glory guards city and plain;
  Brightest emblem of freedom divine!
No foe can her progress restrain
  While the stars in her union shine.
        Hurrah! Hurrah! Hurrah!

Old Glory floats over the wave
  From the poles to the farthest blue sea;
She breaks the foul chains of the slave,
  And proclaims, all mankind shall be free!
        Hurrah! Hurrah! Hurrah!

Old Glory forever shall stand!
 She's the flag of the brave and the true;
The pride of our Heaven-blest land!
 Let us cheer for the red, white and blue!
 Hurrah! Hurrah! Hurrah!

SELF EXAMINATION.

As forth the dawning o'er the east sky broke
Two paths thy early inward choice at once provoke;
One leads to worldly good alone, to ease and pelf;
And one to heights of love, the sacrifice of self.

To choose the road cost tears and anxious thought,
That error might not win what light so sweetly brought;
Missteps, perchance, have marked thy path this day,
While good intentions left their blanks along the way.

Men strive for wealth, and dwell in pleasures vain;
Few live for Heav'n, to prove that life in Christ is gain.
Sufficient earthly good to spare and bless
With sweet content should mark thy highest happiness.

To crave the things of earth for self's desires
Too oft the soul with zealous earnestness aspires,
'Til some bright spark of heavenly flame ignites
The truer life within and Christlike love indites.

This day like many others of its kind
Has gone indeed, and left its memories behind
Of good and evil, conflicts for the right ;
To conquer pride and self was far the greater fight.

The Lord, thy Helper, all thy need supplies.
Thy Guardian and thy Guide where'er the danger lies ;
To pleasant pastures and to waters clear
He leads securely on and thou hast nought to fear.

With grateful thoughts of his abiding Grace
Thou may'st in Jesus each and every blessing trace ;
For, all of good that comes to thee below
Comes through His boundless love whose Name is life to know.

As day by day recedes, blest soul, adore
The loving heart of Jesus Christ yet more and more !
Sweet peace and rest thou'lt share at His right hand
When in His blissful presence thou shalt safely stand.

Unfasten every tie that binds thee here
And for eternal mansions have thy title clear ;
Salvation seek of Him who freely gives,
'Twill be thy joy to know that thy Redeemer lives.

MY EARTHLY HOUSE.

Thy might and majesty I gladly own,
　　Thy right it is to prove me as Thou wilt ;
Set up in this poor tenement Thy throne ;
　　That house endures which on the Rock is built.

A shattered, tempest-beaten hut of clay,
  Once subject to the winds and flood's commands,
Without protection, shield or proper stay,
  Hard by the river's brink of shifting sand.

No sure foundation had, no corner-stone ;
  But wretchedness and guilt without, within ;
There came a Builder, moved by Grace alone,
  Desired possession, claimed it, entered in.

The work of reconstruction then began :
  Down roof and rafters came, partitions, frame ;
Scarce recognition left the wondrous plan ;
  A transformed dwelling hence this hut became.

Now, on the Rock of Ages stayed, no harm
  Is feared, nor danger ; but within, without.
Sweet Comfort, Peace and Joy walk arm in arm.
  While Faith and Love dispel all care and doubt.

Upon the threshold Truth stands sentinel ;
  Virtue and Prudence from the windows look,
While here the blessed Spirit comes to dwell
  And wisdom teaches from His gracious Book.

From stormy winds and lightning flash secure,
  Since Thou art with me, Lord, I fear no ill ;
Thy presence shall my present good insure,
  Thy temple Thou wilt with Thy glory fill.

41

REST.

"There remaineth therefore a rest to the people of God."—Heb. 4. 9.

Perfect rest the Father gives
To the soul that humbly lives
In the sunlight of His grace
As it gleams from Jesus face.

Blest shall be that cherished state
Where all joys shall concentrate
In the love of God supreme
Flowing in perpetual stream.

Jesus will His saints confess,
Clothe them in His righteousness;
Welcome them to feasts of love
In His Father's house above.

All the weary, sin-oppressed
May secure this promised rest;
Nought that harms can enter there,
Death nor sorrow, doubt nor care.

Faith and hope this boon may claim
In the dear Redeemer's Name.
Promised rest! so sweet, so pure!
Which forever shall endure.

When the thread of life is spun
And earth's tedious toils are done,
Then, in heav'nly mansions blest,
Saints shall find their promised rest.

CHRIST OUR REFUGE.

Is there on earth a place
From sin and pain secure?
Some shelter from the ills of life,
A refuge safe and sure?

This world a paradise
Once was ere feeble man
Had sinned! Then death and sorrow came
When Satan's reign began.

The refuge that we need
Is found in Christ alone;
He has, with might and majesty,
The Tempter overthrown.

His armor well protects
The warrior through the fight;
His Spirit guards the weakest saint
That seeks for Heavenly light.

His blood a wall has built
That nothing e'er may pass
To harm His bride, e'en though all hell
His Kingdom should harass.

There's comfort in His love;
There's safety 'neath His wings;
Sweet peace with God, most blessed boon!
The peace His Spirit brings.

Great Hiding-place from death !
　Safe Refuge from distress !
A mighty Rock, impregnable,
　Is Christ, our Righteousness !

His help can never fail ;
　Blest hope beyond the grave !
We'll rest in perfect faith in Him
　And trust His power to save.

Nor shall we trust in vain,
　Since He is all in all ;
For those who in this Refuge hide
　Can from Him never fall.

FORGIVEN.

To be forgiven ! Pardon for the past
Received through ransom paid for debts so vast
That nothing less than Jesus blood could clear
The guilty soul, or bring salvation near.

To the inheritance of sons and heirs
Jehovah calls, and through His word declares
That, by the hearing ear and willing mind
Believing hearts shall his adoption find.

Oh wondrous freedom! Fixed on joys above
The soul rejoicing shares a Saviour's love;
And bringing ev'ry weight of earthly care
And sin to Jesus cross it leaves it there.

'Tis by th' atonement made by Him who died
And lives again, enthroned and glorified.
The penitent finds peace with God, and joy;
While loving deeds henceforth his hands employ.

Oh, peace of pardon! Bliss it is to know
This love of God to mortals here below.
To be forgiven! Washed from sin's deep stain!
Indeed, "to live is Christ, to die is gain."

Within the Kingdom of God's hallowed grace
May every sinner find a refuge-place;
Since holy living must on earth begin
By cleansing of the heart from inbred sin.

From all pollution cleansed and clothed upon
With Christ's own spotless righteousness, anon
Believing saints, with holy thoughts possessed,
Seek new delights with Jesus as their guest.

The vision opens to the scene beyond
Where faithful ones, united by the bond
Of God's redemption, wait the happy day
When Christ shall drive the night of sin away.

What blest anticipation ! Faith takes hold
Of promised mansions, streets of shining gold !
'Twere well to picture such a rest as this ;
The soul forgiven there abides in bliss.

Oh, glorious morn ! Refulgent with the light
That beams divinely from the mountain height
Of God's eternal love ! Oh, hallowed hour
When Christ shall come to claim His own with power !

To be translated from earth's vain desires !
To sing the new, new song in heavenly choirs
In ecstacy of love ! What joys supreme
In God's forgiving mercies ever gleam !

DESIRE.

I want to leave some mark that everyone may see
   Who follows where my pilgrim path has lain.
Such as the woodman blazes on the tree,
   Ere reached the light that shines beyond the gloom and pain.

I want to raise some precious tender flower of earth
   To bloom in bright celestial rich array,
Transcending all resplendent scenes where mirth
   And pleasure unrestrained have held their sceptred sway.

I want to humbly stoop and take some soiled hand
  And lift a soul bowed down with grief and sin.
And guide the straying one toward that loved land
  Where ne'er a sorrow nor a sigh can enter in.

I want to press my hand upon some fevered brow
  And speak a gentle word of holy peace;
To say, Behold thy loving Saviour now.
  'Tis He alone can cause the deepest pain to cease;

It may not be the Heav'nly Father's righteous will
  To take affliction from thee nor thy care;
But Jesus can the wildest billows still
  And give thee patient grace thy hardest lot to bear.

I want no monument of polished granite stone
  To mark the place where I have toiled and trod,
Nor any praise from men nor kingly throne;
  But one in love to say,—" He led me to my God."

Give me the honor to confess that Saving Name
  Before a living world.   That Name of Might!
By men rejected when as man He came
  Our foe to conquer and to set the world aright.

Let me but bear the banner of his love aloft,
  That ruined men may look, believe and live.
On city street or lane, by lowly croft;
  Or ocean-side, where Jesus may His Spirit give.

'Tis well to realize our years on earth are few,
 That we shall stand before the Judgment Seat
Of Christ, the Lamb once slain to pay the sinner's due,
 Who, raised, ascended, glorified, we there shall meet.

I want to see His coming! Lord of lords and King!
 Surrounded by th' Angelic glory-throng!
And, quick or resurrected, may I sing
 Forever and for aye the great Redemption Song.

THE OLD AND THE NEW YEAR.

The earth looks bare and drear ;
 The frost and winter's blast
Have robbed the fields of verdure fair
 And over all is cast
 A strange and mellow gloom !
But soon the sun will lend
 Its rays to paint the scene ;
To give the flowers their various hues,
 To clothe the meads with green.
 And fill the atmosphere with sweet perfume.

To us come wintry hours
 Of care, which bring to nought
The joys and hopes of youthful years,
 When all the good we've sought
 Forever vanished seems !

But light and warmth return
To drive our gloom away ;
New prospects rise to cheer our skies.
New hopes turn night to day,
And o'er our lives peace sheds its rising beams.

"FRIENDSHIP, LOVE AND TRUTH"

Three charming neighbors
Partners through years,
Faithful midst labors,
Trials and tears.

Side by side ever,
Watch they each day ;
Naught can them sever,
Wizzard nor fay.

Friendship for all men
Trustful and kind,
Ready to help when
Sorrow they find.

Love in its beauty
Heals ev'ry woe,
Cherishing duty
Conqu'ring each foe.

49

Truth o'er creation
  Spreads its bright rays,
Teaching the nation
  God's name to prais .

Friendship oft lightens
  Burdens men bear ; ·
Love their path brightens
  Banishing care.

Truth as the morning
  Letteth in light ;
Ignorance scorning,
  Beacon of right.

God's peace attend thee
  Emblem most grand ;
We, to defend thee,
  Pledge heart and hand.

NOTHING GREAT IN ITSELF.

The grains of sand the mountains build,
The mighty sea with drops is filled,
The world of atoms small is made ;
In all God's goodness is displayed.
So. man who dwells beneath the sun
Should little boast what he has done ;
Since nothing great at once appears,
For greatness is the sum of years.

LOOKING FORWARD!

An image I see in yonder tree
Which seems to smile with a happy glee
And ask with eyes that look at me,
" In a hundred years where wilt thou be?"

An angel appears in that bright cloud.
It seems to hover and speak aloud.
It says, " when years thy form have bowed
Will thy soul with glory be endowed?"

A gleaming of light in western sky,
Awhile 'tis bright then it seems to die ;
It tokens blissful rest on high,
For eternity is drawing nigh !

The Pillar of fire that went before
The sons of Jacob the desert o'er
Still lights the way to Heaven's door
Where the saints who enter sigh no more.

A bird in its upward rapid flight
Darts forth for prey to the mountain height
Its happy instinct turns to sight
As it satisfies its appetite.

Behold how the mountains hem me in
Like dungeon walls to the vale of sin ;
But why remain content within ?
There's a prize beyond for me to win !

The twilight o'ershades the forest trees
With gloom enough for such scenes as these;
But nature blends with things that please
The foul upas tree of dread disease.

The evening of life is coming fast,
We plainly see that the sands have past,
The day has fled and darkness cast,
For no earthly good can ever last.

The image well hints that life soon fades;
The angel gently our spirit aids;
God's Light dispels all gloomy shades
And a holy joy our heart pervades.

Our spirit shall mount to glory fair.
Enough of good and a throne to share;
A starry crown the wise shall wear
And the Lord will banish every care.

AN EVENING THOUGHT.

Hast thou spoken a word for the Master to-day?
    Hast thou done a kind deed in His name?
Hast thou made any effort some truth to convey
To the one who has wandered far out of the way,
    The poor sinner Christ came to reclaim?

As the time. than on eagle wing. faster has flown,
  And the hours have passed rapidly by,
Was the Kingdom of God in its glory made known?
Has some pilgrim the pathway to Heaven been shown,
  Or aught done. his great need to supply?

There are thousands, who stand at the doorway without,
  Who are waiting to enter the fold!
Hast thou sought to help one of these overcome doubt,
Or assisted the tempted the tempter to rout?
  Was one name in the Lamb's book enrolled?

A reward shall be given, a crown shall be thine
  If but faithful and true thou wilt prove;
For the wise as the firmament's brightness shall shine,
They that many to righteousness firmly incline
  Bright as stars shall eternally move.

Then arise and be doing the work now at hand,
  For the Master will come for His own!
The redeemed of all Nations together shall stand
Before Jesus. a blood-washed and purified band,
  In the glory that circles His Throne.

CONSECRATION.

Stand firm! The world with splendid show
  Allures thee to desert thy calling;
The pride of life, a subtle foe,
  Attacks thee with a skill appalling.

Stand, fortress-like! Satanic darts
   May never strike thee to thy harming;
God knows thy heart and aye imparts
   Munition full for all thy arming.

Decide for life the course thou'lt take
   And formulate thy plan of living;
Thy solemn purpose ne'er forsake;
   Thyself for others ever giving.

Beware of pitfalls sin has laid;
   Beware the idols set before thee;
The law of God when disobeyed
   Can ne'er to righteousness restore thee.

God's Spirit must His presence lend
   To make of thee a temple holy;
God's love alone a Christ can send
   To make that temple pure and lowly.

Though earth be swayed by tempest shock,
   Though nations crumble, never falter!
A sure foundation is thy Rock
   While burns the incense on God's altar.

"HE WILL COME AGAIN."

When the Master comes in brightness,
   When He comes to call the roll,
In a robe of dazzling whiteness
   He will clothe each ransomed soul.

54

While we're waiting, yet desiring
  Some glad message from above,
He is still our hearts inspiring
  With fresh tokens of his love.

When we sought His gracious blessing
  Blood-bought pardon we received;
In His Name we're now confessing
  The good tidings we believed.

Here we claim no earthly treasure
  For the service done for Him;
Yet our cup with holy pleasure
  He is filling to the brim.

Now we know the wond'rous power
  Of His boundless, loving grace,
Which shall keep us 'til the hour
  We behold Him face to face.

We shall see Him in His glory,
  And remain with Him for aye;
Then we'll chant the " old, old story,"
  In the realms of endless day.

Oh, the blissful, peaceful resting
  That awaits us bye and bye!
Hear the Spirit's voice attesting
  That the day-dawn draweth nigh!

He will come in all His brightness,
He will come to claim His own;
Then, in garbs of spotless whiteness,
We shall stand about His throne.

Joyful hallelujahs ringing,
Grateful homage we will bring;
Saints shall join with angels singing
Praise to Heaven's Eternal King.

"BE YE STEADFAST."

(1 Cor. 15. 58)

We'll be steadfast in the keeping
Of our purpose, souls to win,
Looking forward to the reaping
And the blessed gathering in.

We'll persistent be in serving
Christ, our Lord, with all our power.
Ever faithful, never swerving
From the duty of the hour.

We'll be earnest in our pleading
That the truth may be made plain
To the minds of those we're leading
To the Lamb for sinners slain.

Looking heavenward, glory viewing.
    Keeping Christ before our eyes,
Good pursuing, sin eschewing,
    We, through Him, shall gain the prize.

Thanks to God! for help in raising
    Men from vanity and vice ;
Thanks to God! forever praising
    Christ, the bleeding sacrifice.

CHRISTIAN LOVE.

I long God's truth to know,
    And o'er His word I pray ;
But can the stream of wisdom flow
    If I its course should stay ?

I seek with childish zeal
    For treasure rich and rare ;
O may His Spirit's grace reveal
    Some pearl or diamond fair.

I joy to be with Christ,
    To walk with Him below ;
But if I e'er should break my tryst
    To whom else could I go ?

57

My hope the promise holds
　That I shall find Him near,
And sup with Him while He enfolds
　Me in His arms most dear.

On Jesus all my trust
　Shall ever surely rest ;
He is both merciful and just,
　He knoweth what is best.

I love with strong desire,
　His reigning power I own ;
O may no lurking sinful ire
　My Lord, my King, dethrone.

My heart is fully set
　To do His gracious will ;
O may I ne'er His love forget,
　Nor do my brother ill.

The love for Him I bear
　Shall suffer no decrease ;
But with my brother I must share
　His love till being cease.

WORSHIP.

We have come to worship Jesus,
　And in adoration bow
Low before our gracious Saviour,
　Who vouchsafes to hear us now.

Jesus, Friend of earth-bound sinners,
    Wash away our every stain ;
May our hearts to Thee be opened
    So that Thou may'st in them reign.

May we find Thy great salvation
    And our souls be filled with love ;
May Thy Kingdom here, Lord Jesus,
    Soon be like to Heav'n above.

Prayers ascend, like incense rising,
    For new pardon, grace and peace ;
May Thy Spirit's influence brighten
    All our lives, our faith increase.

May the wisdom of Thy gospel
    Comfort for all times afford,
And may we be waiting ready
    At Thy coming, dearest Lord.

THE CHRIST-CHILD.

Beautiful Christ-child in the manger,
Innocent, holy, lovely " stranger " !
Heralds angelic great joy bringing,
Glory to God from Heaven ringing ;

Peace upon earth, they come fore-telling,
Songs of "good-will to men" are swelling.
Thine be the praise! 'Til time is ended
Heaven and earth in Thee are blended.

Beautiful Christ-child once so humble!
Ruler of Kings as world-thrones crumble!
Victor o'er death and powers infernal!
Lord over all and God eternal.
Angels Thy Name above adoring,
Mortals Thy Grace are still imploring.
Thine be the honor! Thine the glory!
Ransomed ones chant the Christmas story.

VESPERS.

May our hearts be touched and tendered
In this solemn twilight hour!
May our holiest praise be rendered
As we feel the Spirits power!

Like the evening star when sinking
Calm reflecting solar light,
May our lives with Christ's love linking
Shed their influence pure and bright!

May our faith grow stronger, steadier,
As we bow in humble prayer!
May our hearts and hands be readier
Others' heavy loads to bear!

THE HOLY SPIRIT.

O Holy Spirit tune our hearts
To sing the joy that Christ imparts ;
Thy hallowed influence reveal,
And fill our souls with patient zeal.

O clear the clouds and mists that rise
To veil our Saviour from our eyes ;
May love grow strong and doubting cease,
O crown our lives with inward peace.

Abide with us in health or pain,
To comfort, cheer, support, sustain ;
O guard us, guide us and assist
That we temptation may resist.

Shed Thou a light upon the way
That leads to Heaven's eternal day ; .
Refresh us with thy quick'ning love
'Til faith is lost in sight above.

DEVOTION.

Lamb of God, Thy Grace impart,
With Thy Truth fill every heart ;
Christ our Lord, in worship now
At Thy mercy-seat we bow.

Humble sacrifice we bring.
While Thy gracious Name we sing;
Cheerful voices here we raise
Hallelujahs to Thy praise.

Christ, Thy majesty we own,
Seated on the Father's Throne;
In our souls Blest Jesus shine
With Thy precious Light divine.

Holy thoughts and willing hands
To perform Thy law's demands,
Purest words and lovely deeds
Make our lives the best of creeds.

Whether good report or ill
Shall on earth our portion fill,
Christ our Lord, Thy mercy-seat
E'er shall be our sure retreat.

When our service here is o'er.
In bright realms for evermore
Christ our Lord with Thee we'll meet
At Thy Heav'nly mercy-seat.

IT'S ALL IN JESUS.

The Door to heav'n is open wide
   That all may enter in ;
Come. see my Saviour's hands and side ;
   He'll wash you clean from sin.
      There's a Door at the entrance to glory for me,
      That Door is my Jesus who died on the tree.

The Way to Heav'n is straight indeed.
   But all may walk therein ;
My Saviour is a friend in need,
   He'll wash you clean from sin.
      There's a Way to the mansions in glory for me,
      That Way is my Jesus who died on the tree.

The Light illumes the narrow road
   For all who walk therein,
And Jesus bears the sinner's load ;
   He'll wash you clean from sin.
      There's a Light at the pathway to glory for me,
      That Light is my Jesus who died on the tree.

The Life in Christ begun below
   Gives joy and peace within ;
Our Jesus saves from ev'ry woe,
   He'll wash you clean from sin.
      There's Life, life eternal in glory for me,
      That Life is in Jesus who died on the tree.

BENEDICTION.

Go little book, and do thy mission well!
In love thou may'st some straying pilgrim tell
How vice to shun, or stormy passion quell.

Go show the seeker after better light,
The path of duty and the road to right,
And open up life's gospel to his sight.

The world is full of crime and guilt and wrong;
So, tune thy precepts into Christ-like song
To swell the ranks of Jesus' blood-washed throng.

The blessed news of saving grace proclaim
And tell how Christ, the Lamb of God, became
A substitute for all who trust His Name.

Then, when the gath'ring hosts at last shall stand
Before the Judge, who sits at God's right hand,
May some through thee find rest in Beulah-land.

God grant a hundred fold to bless thy seed,
Though simple here thy speech and plain thy creed,
May joys supreme there crown thy loving deed.

www.ingramcontent.com/pod-product-compliance
Lightning Source LLC
Chambersburg PA
CBHW022153020726

47496CB00008B/2689

* 9 7 8 3 3 3 7 3 9 1 8 5 0 *